Christmas in Maine

KAYLA LOWE

Want a free book? Sign up to my newsletter to get my award-winning book for free! www.authorkaylalowe.com

More of My Books

Series

Christmas Blessings

Christmas Miracle for Two
A Christmas Promise of Love
A Christmas of Renewed Faith

Women of the Bible Fiction

Ruth
Esther
Rachel
Hannah
Deborah

Charms of the Chaste Court

A Courtship in Covent Garden
Whispers in Westminster
Romance in Regent's Park
Serenade on Strand Street
Treasure in Tower Bridge

Sweet Honey by the Sea

The Beekeeper's Secret (Book 1)
A Royal Honeycomb (Book 2)
Bees in Blossom (Book 3)
Honeyed Kisses (Book 4)
Blooming Forever (Book 5)

Strawberry Beach Series

Beachside Lessons (Book 1)
Beachside Lessons (Book 2)
Beachside Lessons (Book 3)

Panama City Beach Series

Sun-Kissed Secrets (Book 1)
Sun-Kissed Secrets (Book 2)
Sun-Kissed Secrets (Book 3)

The Tainted Love Saga

Of Love and Deception (Book 1)
Of Love and Family (Book 2)
Of Love and Violence (Book 3)

Of Love and Abuse(Book 4)
Of Love and Crime (Book 5)
Of Love and Addiction (Book 6)
Of Love and Redemption (Book 7)

Standalones

Maiden's Blush

Poetry

Phantom Poetry
Lost and Found

Chapter One

The snow-dusted pines whizzed by as Alexia Beasley's car wound its way down the familiar roads of her childhood. Her heart quickened with each passing landmark, memories of Christmases past flooding her mind. The old general store, now with a fresh coat of red paint, still had the same cheerful wreath on its door.

"Home sweet home," Alexia murmured, her breath fogging up the window. She couldn't help but smile as she turned onto Maple Street, where her parents' house stood proudly at the end of the cul-de-sac.

As she pulled into the driveway, the scent of pine and woodsmoke filled her nostrils. The two-story colonial was adorned with twinkling lights and garland, just as it had been every Christmas she could remember. Alexia's eyes misted over as she took in the sight, overwhelmed by a sense of belonging she hadn't felt in years.

The front door burst open before she could even cut the engine. Her mother rushed out, arms outstretched, with her father following close behind.

"Oh, sweetheart! You're here!" Marilyn exclaimed, enveloping Alexia in a warm embrace that smelled of cinnamon and vanilla.

"Hi, Mom," Alexia laughed, returning the hug fiercely. "Dad, a little help with the bags?"

Henry chuckled, his strong arms already reaching for her suitcases. "Welcome home, pumpkin. Your mother's been baking up a storm all day."

As they made their way inside, Alexia's gaze swept over the familiar entryway. The same wreath of pinecones hung on the wall, and the old grandfather clock in the corner still chimed every quarter-hour.

"Oh, honey, remember how you used to love helping me hang the stockings?" her mother said, gesturing to the fireplace mantel where four red stockings hung in a neat row.

Alexia nodded, a lump forming in her throat. "And Dad would always pretend he couldn't reach the top of the tree to let me put the star on."

Her father's eyes twinkled. "Well, now you're tall enough to do it without any help. Speaking of which, we've got the perfect tree waiting in the living room for you to decorate."

As they settled into the cozy living room, the scent of gingerbread wafted from the kitchen. Alexia sank into the soft cushions of the couch, letting the warmth of home and family wash over her.

"So, tell us all about the big city life," her mother said, settling in beside her daughter. "We want to hear everything."

Alexia smiled, realizing how much she'd missed this—the simple joy of being with her parents, sharing stories, and feeling completely at ease.

“Let her get unpacked first, Marilyn,” her father said with a chuckle.

Alexia gave her father a grateful smile as she headed to her room.

Once there, she unzipped her suitcase, the familiar scent of home mingling with the crisp winter air drifting through the cracked window. As she cleared out a dresser draw, she lifted out a stack of neatly folded sweaters and something small and glittery tumbled onto the patchwork quilt.

"Oh!" she exclaimed, picking up the delicate object. It was a hand-painted glass ornament, a miniature evergreen tree adorned with tiny gold stars. Alexia's breath caught in her throat as memories flooded back.

"I can't believe this is still here," she murmured, turning the ornament gently in her hands. Her mind drifted to Philip Bishop, the boy who had given her this ornament so many Christmases ago.

"Honey, everything okay up there?" her mother's voice called from downstairs.

"Yeah, Mom," Alexia replied, her voice slightly strained. "Just found an old ornament."

She set the ornament on her nightstand, her fingers lingering on its smooth surface. "I wonder what ever happened to you, Philip," she whispered.

Shaking off the wave of nostalgia, Alexia finished unpacking and decided to clear her head with a walk. She bundled up in her favorite peacoat and stepped out into the crisp afternoon air.

The woods behind her parents' house beckoned, a winter wonderland of snow-laden branches and hushed stillness. As Alexia crunched along the familiar path, she felt the tension in her shoulders begin to melt away.

"I'd forgotten how beautiful it is out here," she said softly, her breath forming little clouds in the frosty air. The only sounds were the crunch of snow beneath her boots and the occasional twitter of a brave winter bird.

Alexia paused in a small clearing, tilting her face up to catch a few errant snowflakes on her cheeks. A sense of peace washed over her, filling the empty spaces she hadn't even realized were there.

She closed her eyes and inhaling deeply. The scent of pine and winter air filled her lungs, grounding her in a way the bustling city never could.

As she stood there, Alexia felt a quiet certainty settle in her heart. Whatever challenges lay ahead, whatever decisions she faced, this place—these woods—would always be a part of her.

She continued walking, enjoying reconnecting with nature when she rounded a bend in the path and collided with a solid figure, letting out a startled "Oof!"

"Whoa there!" A deep, warm voice chuckled. "Are you okay?"

Alexia looked up, her eyes widening in recognition. "Philip? Philip Bishop?"

Philip's green eyes crinkled with surprise and delight. "Alexia Beasley? Is that really you?"

For a moment, they stood frozen, the years stretching between them like a chasm. Alexia's heart raced, a mix of awkwardness and excitement coursing through her.

"I...wow," she stammered, tucking a strand of hair behind her ear. "It's been so long."

Philip's easy smile broke the tension. "Too long. What brings you back to our winter wonderland?"

As they fell into step together, Alexia found herself relaxing. "Oh, you know, the usual holiday homecoming. How about you? Still running the family tree farm?"

Philip nodded, his expression a mix of pride and something more complex. "Sure am. It's a lot of work, but there's something special about being part of people's Christmas traditions."

Alexia thought back to the ornament she'd found earlier. "I was just thinking about you, actually. Remember that Christmas ornament you gave me in fourth grade?"

Philip's laugh echoed through the trees. "How could I forget? You were the first girl I gave a Christmas gift to—you know, that I wasn't related to."

“I found it stuffed in a drawer in my room just now.”

Philip grinned.

As they walked and talked, Alexia found herself

studying Philip. He'd grown into his lanky frame, his shoulders broad beneath his warm jacket. But his eyes were the same—kind, with that spark of mischief she remembered so well.

"So, what's new in the big city?" Philip asked, his tone genuinely interested.

Alexia hesitated, unsure how to sum up years of life in a few sentences. "Oh, you know...work, friends, the usual. But being back here...it's making me realize how much I've missed this place."

Philip's gaze softened. "Well, we've missed you too, Lex. The town's not quite the same without its resident troublemaker."

Alexia laughed, feeling a warmth that had nothing to do with her winter coat. "Troublemaker? I seem to recall a certain someone who was always dragging me into his schemes."

As they continued to reminisce and catch up, Alexia felt the last of her nervousness melt away. There was something comforting about talking with Philip, like slipping on a favorite sweater she'd forgotten she owned.

Chapter Two

The crackle of the fireplace filled the cozy living room as Alexia settled into the plush armchair, cradling a mug of hot cocoa. Across from her, Philip lounged on the sofa, his lanky frame relaxed as he sipped his own drink. The familiar comfort of being in each other's presence after so many years apart warmed Alexia's heart.

"So, Ms. Big City Marketing Specialist," Philip teased, his green eyes twinkling, "tell me all about the glamorous life you've been living since high school."

Alexia laughed, the sound echoing off the wooden beams above. "Oh, you know, just living the dream of staring at spreadsheets and creating PowerPoint presentations."

As she spoke about her job, Alexia found herself

watching Philip's reactions, noticing how his smile never wavered. *Has he always been this attentive?* she wondered, a flutter of something unfamiliar stirring in her chest.

"But enough about me," she said, leaning forward. "What about you? Running the family farm must be quite the adventure."

Philip's expression softened, a mix of pride and weariness crossing his features. "It's challenging, but rewarding. Every day brings something new."

"I bet," Alexia nodded, memories of their childhood escapades on the farm flooding back. "Remember when we tried to sneak that baby pine tree into my bedroom?"

Philip burst out laughing, nearly spilling his cocoa. "How could I forget? Your mom's face when she found dirt all over your carpet!"

As they reminisced, trading stories and laughter, Alexia felt a warmth spreading through her that had nothing to do with the fire or her drink. It was like no time had passed at all.

Suddenly, Philip sat up straighter, his eyes lighting up with an idea. "Hey, speaking of the farm, I could really use an extra pair of hands this season. Any chance you'd want to help out while you're in town?"

Alexia's heart skipped a beat. Spending more time with Philip? On the beautiful farm where they'd shared so many memories? "I'd love to," she replied, her smile mirroring his own. "It'll be just like old times."

As Philip began excitedly outlining his plans for the season, Alexia found herself swept up in his enthusiasm. She realized that coming home for Christmas might turn out to be the best decision she'd made in years.

Alexia's boots crunched through the fresh snow as she followed Philip down a winding path between rows of fragrant pine trees. The crisp winter air nipped at her cheeks, but she felt warm inside, invigorated by the beauty surrounding her and Philip's infectious enthusiasm.

"So, what made you decide to take over the farm?" Alexia asked, her breath forming small clouds in the air. "I remember you talking about becoming a teacher back in high school."

Philip paused, his green eyes thoughtful as he gazed at the snow-capped trees. "I did consider teaching for a while," he admitted. "But there's something about this place, you know? It's not just a business. It's a part of who I am."

Alexia nodded, understanding all too well the pull of home and tradition. "I get that. Sometimes I wonder if I made the right choice moving to the city for my career."

"Do you regret it?" Philip asked softly.

"No...not exactly," Alexia said, her brow furrowing slightly. "I love my job, but sometimes I feel like I'm missing out on something here. Like I'm not living up to expectations."

Philip's warm hand on her arm stopped her. "Hey, you're doing amazing things, Lex. Your family is proud of you, I'm sure of it."

Alexia felt a flutter in her chest at his words and the sincerity in his eyes. "Thanks, Phil. So, what's this project you need help with?"

Philip's face lit up. "Come on, I'll show you!"

He led her to a clearing where a half-finished wooden structure stood. "I'm building a new display area for our handmade wreaths and ornaments," he explained. "Think you can help me hang these strings of lights?"

As they worked side by side, stringing twinkling lights across the beams, Alexia found herself stealing glances at Philip. The way his face creased in concentration, the gentle strength in his hands as he secured each strand—it all felt so familiar yet new at the same time.

"You know," Philip said, breaking the comfortable silence, "I've always admired how you chase after your dreams, Lex. It takes courage to leave everything you know behind."

Alexia paused, touched by his words. "Sometimes I wonder if I'm chasing the right dreams," she confessed.

As the sun began to set, casting a golden glow across the snow-covered landscape, Alexia and Philip stood back to admire their handiwork. The lights twinkled softly, creating a magical atmosphere in the clearing.

"It's beautiful," Alexia breathed, taking in the scene.

"Yeah, it is," Philip agreed softly, but when Alexia turned, she found him looking at her instead of the lights. Their eyes met, and for a moment, the world seemed to stand still.

Alexia's heart fluttered as she met Philip's gaze, a blush creeping up her cheeks. She quickly looked away, focusing on adjusting a string of lights that didn't need adjusting.

"So," she said, her voice a touch higher than

usual, "remember when we used to decorate the treehouse with tinsel and mom's old ornaments?"

Philip chuckled, leaning against one of the wooden beams. "How could I forget? You always insisted on hanging that ratty old star at the top."

"Hey!" Alexia protested, playfully swatting his arm. "That star was a family heirloom."

"A heirloom that looked like it had been through a paper shredder," Philip teased, his eyes twinkling with mirth.

Alexia couldn't help but laugh, the sound bubbling up from deep within her. It felt so natural, so right to be here with Philip like this. As their laughter subsided, she found herself wondering what it might be like if...

No, she couldn't let herself go down that path. She was leaving after Christmas, back to her life in the city. But the way Philip was looking at her now, with such warmth and affection, made her heart ache with possibility.

"You know," Philip said softly, taking a step closer, "I've really missed this. Missed you."

Alexia's breath caught in her throat. "I've missed you too," she admitted, her voice barely above a whisper.

For a moment, they stood there, the air between

them charged with unspoken feelings. Alexia's mind raced. Was this really happening? Did she want it to happen?

Before she could decide, Philip cleared his throat and took a step back. "We should probably head back. It's getting dark."

Alexia nodded, both relieved and disappointed. As they walked back to the farmhouse, their hands brushed occasionally, sending little sparks through her body. She couldn't deny the excitement bubbling up inside her, but it was tinged with confusion. What did this mean for her carefully laid plans?

As they reached the porch, Philip turned to her with a smile. "Same time tomorrow?"

"Wouldn't miss it," Alexia replied, her heart skipping a beat at the prospect.

She watched him walk away, her emotions swirling like the gently falling snow around her. One thing was certain—this Christmas was turning out to be far more complicated, and far more magical, than she had ever anticipated.

Chapter Three

The soft glow of candlelight illuminated the faces of the congregation as Alexia sat beside her parents in the familiar wooden pew. The scent of pine and cinnamon filled the air, mingling with the reverent voices singing "O Little Town of Bethlehem." Alexia's heart swelled with emotion as she joined in, her clear soprano rising above the melody.

As the final notes faded, Pastor Mike stepped up to the pulpit, his kind eyes twinkling. "Today we gather to remember the greatest gift of all—the birth of our Savior," he began.

Alexia found herself leaning forward, drinking in every word. The pastor's message about love, hope, and redemption resonated deeply within her. She glanced at her mother, noticing the tears glistening in her eyes.

I needed this reminder, Alexia thought, feeling a weight lift from her shoulders. *It's so easy to get caught up in the chaos and forget what truly matters.*

As the service concluded, Alexia hugged her parents tightly. "That was beautiful," she murmured. "Thank you for bringing me."

Her father squeezed her hand. "We're glad you could join us, sweetheart."

Alexia's heart warmed at his words. As they made their way down the aisle, she caught sight of a familiar face. Philip stood near the entrance, his green eyes lighting up when he saw her.

"Alexia!" he called out, weaving through the crowd to reach her.

"Philip," she replied, feeling a flutter in her stomach. "I didn't expect to see you here."

He rubbed the back of his neck, a shy smile playing on his lips. "I don't usually attend, but something drew me here today. I'm glad I came—Pastor Mike's message really struck a chord."

Alexia nodded enthusiastically. "It was powerful, wasn't it? I feel like I needed that reminder of what Christmas is truly about."

Philip's expression grew thoughtful. "You know, I've been doing a lot of soul-searching lately."

Alexia felt a surge of warmth at his openness. "Me too," she said softly.

Philip's face lit up. "Hey, Would you like to grab a cup of hot chocolate and talk?"

"I'd like that very much," she replied with a smile. Philip offered her his arm.

As they walked out into the crisp night air, Alexia felt a sense of peace settle over her.

It would be nice to reconnect with Philip more.

As they sipped their hot chocolates, the warmth spreading through their hands, Alexia's eyes lit up with an idea. "Philip, you know what would really embody the spirit of Christmas? Volunteering at the local shelter. They're always short-handed this time of year."

Philip's green eyes sparkled with enthusiasm. "That's a fantastic idea! I've been meaning to give back more to the community. When were you thinking?"

"How about tomorrow evening?" Alexia

suggested, her heart racing with excitement. "They serve dinner at six."

"Count me in," Philip replied with a grin. "I'll pick you up at five-thirty?"

The next evening, as they walked into the bustling shelter, the scent of hearty stew filled the air. Alexia felt a mix of nerves and anticipation as she tied on her apron. "I hope we can make a difference," she murmured.

Philip squeezed her shoulder gently. "We will. Every little bit helps."

As they began serving, Alexia couldn't help but marvel at Philip's natural ease. He chatted warmly with each person, remembering names and asking about their days. His kindness seemed to brighten the whole room.

"How're you holding up?" Philip asked, refilling the bread basket.

Alexia smiled, feeling a warmth that had nothing to do with the steam rising from the serving trays. "I'm good. This feels...right, you know?"

As the evening progressed, Alexia found herself stealing glances at Philip. The way he knelt to speak to a child at eye level, the gentleness with which he helped an elderly man to his seat—each action made her heart swell with admiration.

They worked hard, but it felt good to both of them, and as the last of the guests filed out, Alexia and Philip found themselves alone in the shelter's small kitchen, washing dishes side by side. The clink of plates and the soft splash of soapy water filled the comfortable silence between them.

Alexia glanced at Philip, noticing the pensive look on his face. "Penny for your thoughts?" she asked, nudging him gently with her elbow.

Philip sighed, his green eyes meeting hers. "You know, being here tonight...it's made me realize how much I've been struggling with my faith lately."

Alexia's hands stilled in the sink. "Really? I never would have guessed. You always seem so...sure."

He chuckled softly, but there was a hint of sadness in it. "Appearances can be deceiving, I guess. It's just...sometimes I wonder if I'm living up to what God wants for me."

Alexia felt a surge of empathy. "I understand that feeling all too well," she admitted, her voice barely above a whisper. "Sometimes the weight of expectations—from family, from my boss—it's overwhelming."

Philip nodded, reaching for another plate. "Exactly. Like, I love the farm, but there's a part of me that wonders if there's something more out there for me. Does that make me ungrateful?"

"I don't think so," Alexia replied, her brow furrowing in thought. "I think...maybe God gives us these desires for a reason. The tricky part is figuring out what that reason is."

As they continued to work, Alexia found herself opening up about her own struggles—the pressure to measure up and be successful, the fear of disappointing her family if she chose a different path.

"It's like I'm caught between two worlds sometimes," she confessed, wiping her hands on a dishtowel. "The Alexia everyone expects me to be, and the Alexia I think I might want to be."

Philip's hand found hers, giving it a gentle squeeze. "I think the Alexia you are right now is pretty amazing," he said softly, his eyes crinkling with warmth.

Alexia felt her cheeks flush, a mixture of embarrassment and something deeper, something she wasn't quite ready to name. "Thanks, Phil," she murmured. "I think you're pretty amazing too."

As they finished cleaning up, a comfortable silence settled between them, filled with newfound understanding and shared vulnerability. Alexia realized that in opening up about their struggles, they had strengthened not just their faith, but their connection to each other.

Chapter Four

The crisp winter air nipped at Alexia's cheeks as she stood beside Philip, gazing at the snow-covered hill before them. Her heart fluttered with excitement, memories of childhood winters flooding back.

"What do you say we relive our youth a bit?" Philip's green eyes sparkled with mischief as he gestured toward the hill. "I bet I can still beat you to the bottom."

Alexia's competitive spirit ignited. "Oh, you're on, Bishop. But don't come crying to me when you're eating my snow dust."

They trudged up the hill, their boots crunching in the fresh powder. Alexia's breath came out in small puffs, reminding her of the dragons she used to imagine herself as a child. At the top, Philip offered her a wooden sled with a gallant bow.

"Your chariot, m'lady," he said with a wink.

Alexia laughed, accepting it with a curtsy. "Why thank you, kind sir. Now prepare to lose spectacularly."

They positioned themselves at the crest of the hill, the anticipation building. Alexia's heart raced, a mix of adrenaline and joy coursing through her veins.

"On three," Philip called out. "One...two..."

Before he could say "three," Alexia pushed off, careening down the hill with a whoop of delight. She heard Philip's surprised laugh behind her as he scrambled to catch up.

The cold wind whipped through her hair as she sped down the slope, the world a blur of white around her. For a moment, she was transported back to her childhood, free from adult worries and responsibilities.

At the bottom, she tumbled off her sled, breathless and giddy. Philip arrived seconds later, playfully tackling her into a snowbank.

"Cheater!" he accused, his face inches from hers, both of them laughing.

"All's fair in love and sledding," Alexia retorted, her cheeks flushed from more than just the cold.

They made their way back to Philip's truck, where he produced a thermos of hot cocoa from a small cooler.

"You came prepared," Alexia noted, gratefully accepting a steaming mug.

Philip shrugged, a shy smile playing on his lips. "I may have been planning this little adventure."

As they sipped their cocoa, Alexia found herself studying Philip's profile. She wondered how she had never noticed the gentle curve of his jaw or the way his eyes crinkled when he smiled.

"You know," Philip said softly, breaking into her thoughts, "I've missed this. Us, I mean. Just hanging out, having fun like we used to."

Alexia's heart skipped a beat. "Me too," she admitted, surprised by the depth of emotion in her own voice.

They sat in comfortable silence, the steam from their cocoa mingling in the cold air. Alexia couldn't help but feel that something had shifted between them, like a long-dormant seed finally beginning to sprout.

The bell above the door chimed merrily as Alexia and Philip stepped into Sweet Memories Bakery. The warm scent of cinnamon and freshly baked bread enveloped them, a stark contrast to the crisp winter air outside.

"Oh my goodness," Alexia breathed, her eyes widening at the display case filled with colorful pastries. "Is that Mrs. Mabel's famous apple pie?"

Philip grinned, leaning in close. "The very same. Some things never change in this town."

They approached the counter, where a plump, friendly woman greeted them. "Philip Bishop! And is that little Alexia Beasley? My, how you've grown!"

Alexia felt a rush of warmth at being recognized. "It's wonderful to see you, Mrs. Mabel. Your bakery smells just as heavenly as I remember."

As they settled into a cozy corner booth with their treats, Alexia took a bite of her apple pie and closed her eyes in bliss. "Mmm, this tastes like childhood."

Philip chuckled, his own plate piled high with sugar cookies. "Remember when we used to save our allowance just to buy these?"

"How could I forget?" Alexia said, her eyes twinkling. "You always insisted on getting one of each flavor."

They fell into easy conversation, reminiscing about their favorite sweets and the trouble they'd get into as kids. Alexia found herself captivated by the way Philip's eyes lit up as he spoke, the gentle timbre of his voice wrapping around her like a warm blanket.

As Philip recounted a particularly funny story about a failed attempt at baking, Alexia felt a sudden pang in her chest. She realized, with a mixture of excitement and trepidation, that her feelings for Philip were growing beyond mere friendship.

Her smile faltered slightly as she thought of how she'd have to go back to the city after Christmas.

"Alexia?" Philip's voice broke through her reverie. "You okay? You looked lost in thought for a moment there."

Alexia forced a bright smile, pushing her worries aside for now. "Just savoring every moment," she said, hoping he couldn't hear the slight tremor in her voice. "After all, I don't know when I'll get to taste Mrs. Mabel's pie again."

Philip's eyes softened as he gazed at Alexia, the warm glow of the Christmas lights reflecting in his green irises. He took a deep breath, as if steeling himself for something important.

"Alexia," he began, his voice low and earnest, "there's something I need to tell you."

Alexia's heart quickened, her fingers unconsciously tightening around her mug of hot cocoa. "What is it, Philip?"

He reached across the table, gently taking her free hand in his. The warmth of his touch sent a jolt through her.

"I never forgot about you," Philip confessed, his words tumbling out in a rush. "All these years, even when you left for the city, you were always there in the back of my mind."

Alexia's breath caught in her throat. She searched his face, finding nothing but sincerity in his expression.

"Really?" she whispered, her heart thumping.

Philip nodded, a shy smile tugging at his lips. "Really. I've always wondered what might have been if we'd stayed in touch."

Alexia's mind raced, a mix of excitement and anxiety swirling within her. *I have to leave after Christmas. This isn't fair to him.*

Out loud, she managed to say, "I...I don't know what to say, Philip. I'm touched, truly. But..."

"But you're leaving," he finished for her, his smile

tinged with sadness. "I know. I just needed you to know how I felt."

The air between them crackled with possibility and unspoken words. Alexia found herself torn between the desire to explore these feelings and the practical reality of her life back in the city.

Just then Mrs. Mabel came over to check on them, and it couldn't be a more welcome reprieve from a conversation that had turned awkward.

Chapter Five

The aroma of cinnamon and pine filled the cozy living room as Alexia helped her mother hang garlands along the fireplace mantel. Outside, snow fell gently, blanketing the quaint Maine town in a festive white.

"You know, sweetheart," her mother began, a familiar tone in her voice that made Alexia's shoulders tense, "your father and I were talking the other day about how lovely it would be to have grandchildren running around here at Christmastime."

Alexia fumbled with the garland, nearly dropping an ornament. "Mom, please," she sighed, forcing a smile. "Can we not do this right now?"

Her father chimed in from his armchair, peering

over his reading glasses. "We just want to see you settled, honey. You're not getting any younger, you know."

A knot formed in Alexia's stomach. She loved her parents dearly, but their not-so-subtle hints about her future were becoming more frequent and harder to ignore.

"I know you mean well," Alexia said, trying to keep her voice light, "but I'm happy with where I am in life right now. My career is going great, and I—"

"Of course, dear," her mother interjected, patting Alexia's hand. "We're so proud of your accomplishments. We just worry about you being alone."

Alexia's mind drifted to Philip, his kind green eyes and warm smile flashing in her thoughts. She felt a blush creep up her cheeks.

"I'm not alone, Mom," she said softly. "I have you, Dad, my friends..."

Her father set down his newspaper. "That's not quite the same thing, pumpkin. Don't you want a family of your own someday?"

Alexia bit her lip, weighing her words carefully. "Of course I do, but these things take time. I can't just snap my fingers and make it happen."

Later that evening, as Alexia helped her mother

with the dishes, she found herself unable to hold back any longer.

"Mom," she began hesitantly, "can I talk to you about something?"

Her mother's eyes softened. "Of course, sweetheart. What's on your mind?"

Alexia took a deep breath. "It's about Philip. I...I think I might have feelings for him."

A knowing smile spread across her mother's face. "Oh, honey. I had a feeling there might be something there."

"Really?" Alexia asked, surprised.

Her mother nodded. "A mother always knows. And Philip is such a wonderful young man. The way he looks at you...well, let's just say I've seen that look before."

Alexia's heart fluttered. "But he has his commitment to his family's farm, and I have my life in the city...Our friendship?"

Her mother took Alexia's hands in hers. "Sweetheart, life is too short to let fear hold you back. If Philip makes your heart sing, then you owe it to yourself to explore those feelings."

Alexia felt a weight lift from her shoulders. "Thanks, Mom. I'm just scared of ruining what we have."

"Love is always a risk," her mother said gently. "But it's one worth taking. Follow your heart, Alexia. It won't lead you astray."

As they finished the dishes, Alexia's mind raced with possibilities.

Philip stood at the edge of the Christmas tree farm, his breath visible in the crisp winter air. The scent of pine surrounded him as he surveyed the rows of trees, each one a testament to years of hard work and dedication. His father's voice cut through the stillness.

"Son, we need to talk about the future of the farm," Mr. Bishop said, his tone serious.

Philip's stomach tightened. "What's on your mind, Dad?"

"We're falling behind, Philip. The big box stores are undercutting us, and we're barely breaking even." His father's weathered face creased with worry.

"Maybe we should consider selling," Philip broached the subject tentatively.

His father reeled back like Philip had punched him in the gut. "Sell? Son, this farm has been in our family for generations."

"I know, Dad. But times are changing. We need to be practical."

His father's look of disappointment cut straight to his heart. "This farm isn't just land and trees. It's your heritage, your future. I have some ideas to modernize, maybe partner with local businesses for events."

Philip sighed and nodded. "Sure, you know I'll help however I can."

As his father walked away, Philip's gaze fell on the old barn where he and Alexia had shared so many childhood memories. The weight of expectation pressed down on him.

Later that evening, Philip met Alexia at their favorite coffee shop in town. The warmth inside was a stark contrast to the chill in his heart.

"Hey," Alexia said, her smile fading as she noticed his troubled expression. "What's wrong?"

Philip ran a hand through his hair. "The farm is struggling. We can't compete anymore, and Dad's too stubborn to sell."

Alexia's eyes widened. "Oh, Philip. I'm so sorry. What are you going to do?"

"I don't know," he admitted, his voice heavy. "I know Dad wants to save it, but I'm not sure how. He's always wanted me to take over..."

"What do you want, though?" Alexia asked softly.

Philip blinked before he admitted slowly, "I honeslty don't know. I've never really thought about it. It was just always understood I would take over the tree farm."

Alexia reached across the table and took Philip's hand, her touch warm and comforting. "You have to follow your own path, Philip. Your father will understand, even if it takes time."

Philip squeezed her hand gratefully, his green eyes finding solace in her blue ones. "You're probably right. I just don't want to let him down, you know?"

Alexia nodded, understanding all too well the weight of family expectations. "I do know. My parents have been dropping not-so-subtle hints about me settling down and starting a family."

Philip's brow furrowed with concern. "That's a lot of pressure. I'm sorry, Lex."

She shrugged, trying to downplay the heaviness in her heart. "It's okay. I know they mean well, but sometimes I feel like I'm suffocating under the weight of their hopes for me."

"I get that," Philip said, his thumb absently tracing circles on the back of her hand. "It's like we're both stuck in these roles that have been written for us, but they don't quite fit."

Alexia sighed, leaning back in her chair. "Exactly. And I'm scared that if I deviate from the script, I'll disappoint everyone."

Philip's gaze softened. "You could never disappoint me, Lex. No matter what path you choose."

Alexia's heart swelled with affection for the man sitting across from her. "Same goes for you, Philip. I'll always be in your corner."

They sat in comfortable silence for a moment, their hands still entwined, drawing strength from each other's presence.

"We'll figure this out together," Philip said finally, his voice filled with quiet determination. "I promise."

Alexia smiled, feeling a glimmer of hope amidst the uncertainty.

As they finished their coffee and stepped out into the snowy night, Alexia looped her arm through Philip's, leaning into his solid warmth. The future may have been unclear, but one thing was certain—they had each other, and somehow, that made everything seem a little more manageable.

He smiled, his eyes crinkling at the corners. "Let's

make a pact. No matter what happens with our families or our careers, we'll always be there for each other. Deal?"

Alexia grinned, holding out her pinky. "Pinky promise."

Philip laughed, linking his pinky with hers.

Chapter Six

Alexia's hands trembled as she clutched the crisp white envelope. The company logo glinted in the warm glow of her desk lamp, a beacon of opportunity. She took a deep breath, savoring the earthy scent of pine that lingered on her sweater from her visit to Philip's farm earlier that day.

"I did it," she whispered, a smile tugging at her lips even as her heart constricted. The promotion she'd worked so hard for was finally hers. Senior Marketing Manager. In the city. Miles away from the quaint town she called home.

Miles away from Philip.

Alexia's mind wandered to his kind green eyes, his gentle laugh. The way he always smelled of fresh evergreens and cinnamon. She shook her head, trying to focus on the excitement of her achievement.

Rising from her desk, she grabbed her coat and headed out into the crisp winter air. Snow crunched beneath her boots as she made her way to the Bishop Christmas Tree Farm, fairy lights twinkling in the distance.

Philip was stacking firewood when she arrived, his cheeks flushed from exertion. He looked up, his face breaking into a wide grin. "Alexia! What brings you by so late?"

She held up the envelope, her voice wavering slightly. "I got some news today."

Philip set down the log he was holding, giving her his full attention. "Good news, I hope?"

Alexia nodded, her blue eyes shining with a mix of excitement and trepidation. "I got the promotion."

"That's fantastic!" Philip exclaimed, enveloping her in a warm hug. But as he pulled away, Alexia noticed the flicker of sadness in his eyes.

"Congratulations, Lex. You deserve it," he said softly, his smile not quite reaching his eyes.

Alexia's heart clenched. "Thank you, Philip. I'm excited..." she trailed off, unsure how to express the tumult of emotions swirling inside her.

Philip was quiet for a moment, his hand absently running through his hair. When he spoke, his voice was thick with emotion. "Well, we'll just have to make these next few weeks extra special then, won't we?"

Alexia looked up, meeting his gaze. The warmth and sincerity she found there made her breath catch. "I'd like that," she murmured, her heart torn between the joy of her accomplishment and the ache of leaving this place—and Philip—behind.

Philip trudged through the snow-covered field, the scent of pine heavy in the crisp winter air. He paused, leaning against a towering evergreen, his green eyes scanning the rows of Christmas trees stretching out before him. The farm had been his family's legacy for generations, but today, it felt more like a burden than a blessing.

"Hey, son!" his father's voice boomed across the field. "How's it looking out there?"

Philip forced a smile, pushing down the knot of anxiety in his stomach. "Looking good, Dad. Plenty of trees ready for the holiday rush."

As his father approached, Philip's mind raced.

How could he tell the man who'd poured his heart and soul into this land that his own son didn't want to carry on the tradition?

"That's my boy," his father said, clapping him on the shoulder. "You'll do great things with this place, Philip. I just know it."

Philip swallowed hard, guilt weighing heavy on his chest. "Thanks, Dad," he managed, his voice barely above a whisper.

Later that evening, Philip found himself sitting on the porch swing, lost in thought. The soft crunch of footsteps in the snow alerted him to Alexia's approach.

"Penny for your thoughts?" she asked, settling beside him.

Philip sighed, running a hand through his hair. "Just...thinking about the future, I guess."

Alexia tilted her head, her blue eyes filled with concern. "Want to talk about it?"

"I don't know, Lex," Philip admitted, his voice heavy with uncertainty. "I've always known I was supposed to take over the farm, but lately...I'm not sure it's what I want anymore."

Alexia reached out, taking his hand in hers. "Have you talked to your dad about this?"

Philip shook his head, his chest tightening at the

thought. "How can I? This farm is everything to him. I can't bear the thought of disappointing him."

"Oh, Philip," Alexia said softly, squeezing his hand. "Your happiness matters too, you know."

As they sat in companionable silence, Philip couldn't help but wonder what path his future would take—and how he wished that Alexia would be a part of it.

Chapter Seven

The heavy wooden door of St. Nicholas Church creaked open, sending a shiver down Alexia's spine. The familiar scent of candle wax and pine boughs enveloped her as she stepped inside, her footsteps echoing in the empty sanctuary.

Alexia made her way down the center aisle, drinking in the sight of twinkling Christmas lights draped along the pews and the majestic evergreen standing proudly near the altar. Her heart swelled with a bittersweet ache of nostalgia.

"Oh Lord," she whispered, sinking onto a worn wooden pew, "I could really use some guidance right about now."

She closed her eyes, allowing the peace of the

sacred space to wash over her. The gentle flicker of candlelight danced behind her eyelids as she poured out her heart in silent prayer.

"I feel so torn," Alexia admitted aloud, her voice barely above a whisper. "I love my new job, but being back home...it just feels right somehow."

As if in response, a gust of wind rattled the stained glass windows, startling her. Alexia's eyes flew open, her gaze drawn to the colorful depiction of the nativity scene above. A faint smile tugged at her lips as she remembered the countless Christmas pageants she'd participated in as a child, right here in this very church.

"I guess some things never change," she mused, running her hand along the smooth, worn wood of the pew.

Meanwhile, across town, Philip Bishop trudged through the freshly fallen snow, his breath visible in the crisp night air. The weight of responsibility pressed heavily on his shoulders as he made his way towards St. Nicholas Church, seeking solace in the only place he knew he could find it.

As he approached the familiar white steeple,

Philip paused, taking in the sight of the old church adorned with twinkling lights. A memory of caroling with Alexia on these very steps flashed through his mind, bringing a wistful smile to his face.

"Lord, I could use a little Christmas miracle right about now," he murmured, reaching for the door handle.

The heavy wooden door creaked open, and Philip stepped inside, shaking the snow from his boots. The soft glow of candlelight illuminated the church's interior, casting long shadows across the nave. His eyes adjusted to the dim light, and he froze in place, his heart skipping a beat.

There, kneeling in the front pew, was Alexia.

Philip's breath caught in his throat. He hadn't expected to see her here, especially not at this hour. He hesitated, unsure whether to disturb her or quietly slip away.

Alexia must have sensed his presence because she turned, her blue eyes widening in surprise. "Philip?" she whispered, her voice echoing softly in the empty church.

"I'm sorry," he said quickly, taking a step back. "I didn't mean to interrupt."

Alexia shook her head, a gentle smile spreading

across her face. "No, it's okay. I was just...thinking. Praying."

Philip moved closer, his footsteps echoing on the stone floor. "Me too," he admitted, sliding into the pew beside her. "Seems like we both had the same idea tonight."

They sat in companionable silence for a moment, the flickering candlelight casting a warm glow on their faces. Philip couldn't help but notice how the soft light made Alexia's chestnut hair shine, bringing out the warmth in her eyes.

"It's funny," Alexia said softly, breaking the silence. "Being back here, it's like no time has passed at all."

Philip nodded, his eyes roaming over the familiar surroundings. "I know what you mean. Remember the Christmas pageant when we were kids? You were the angel, and I was—"

"The grumpy innkeeper," Alexia finished, giggling. "How could I forget? You were so nervous, you almost forgot to turn Mary and Joseph away."

They both laughed, the sound of their mirth filling the sacred space. As their laughter subsided, Philip felt a surge of emotion well up inside him. Here, in this place that held so many memories, he suddenly knew he couldn't hold back any longer.

"Alexia," he said, his voice thick with emotion. "I need to tell you something."

She turned to face him, her expression curious and open. "What is it, Philip?"

He took a deep breath, his heart pounding. "I...I love you, Alexia. I think I always have."

Alexia's eyes widened, her breath catching in her throat. The church suddenly felt both impossibly large and incredibly intimate. She opened her mouth to speak, but words failed her.

Philip, sensing her hesitation, gently took her hand. "I know this is a lot to take in," he said softly, his green eyes filled with sincerity. "And I understand you have a life in the city now."

Alexia's mind raced, torn between the warmth of Philip's touch and the memory of her hard-earned career. "Philip, I...I care for you too, but my job..."

He squeezed her hand reassuringly. "I don't want to pressure you to move back home, Alexia. I know how hard you've worked for your new position."

Relief washed over her face, mingled with a hint of confusion. "But what about us? What about the tree farm?"

Philip's lips curved into a gentle smile. "I was thinking...maybe we could try a long-distance relationship? At least until I figure out what to do about the farm."

Alexia's blue eyes sparkled with hope. "You'd be willing to do that?"

"Of course," Philip nodded, his voice warm. "You're worth it, Alexia. We can make this work, one step at a time."

Alexia felt a weight lift from her shoulders. She gazed at Philip, seeing the boy she grew up with and the man he'd become. Without a word, she leaned in, closing the distance between them.

Their lips met in a soft, tender kiss. It felt like coming home and embarking on a new adventure all at once. As they parted, both slightly breathless, Alexia whispered, "Yes, let's make this work."

The candlelight flickered, casting dancing shadows on the church walls, as if celebrating their new beginning.

Chapter Eight

Alexia's hands trembled slightly as she held out the carefully wrapped gift to Philip. The twinkling lights of the Christmas tree cast a warm glow over his face, highlighting the anticipation in his green eyes.

"I hope you like it," she said softly, her heart fluttering as their fingers brushed during the exchange.

Philip grinned, the corners of his eyes crinkling. "I'm sure I'll love it, Lex. But you first—open mine."

Alexia carefully untied the red ribbon on the small box he handed her, savoring the moment. As she lifted the lid, she gasped. Inside was a delicate silver cross necklace, glittering with tiny crystals.

"Oh, Philip, it's beautiful," she breathed, overcome with emotion. How perfect for him to get her a gift that shared their faith.

"Here, let me," Philip offered, gently fastening the necklace around her neck. His warm breath tickled her skin, sending a shiver down her spine.

Now it was Philip's turn. He tore into the wrapping with boyish enthusiasm, revealing a leather-bound photo album. As he flipped through the pages, his eyes widened.

"These are all pictures of us as kids," he said in awe. "How did you get these?"

Alexia blushed. "I may have enlisted our moms' help. I wanted to capture all those special moments."

Philip pulled her into a tight embrace. "It's perfect. You're perfect," he murmured into her hair.

As they reluctantly pulled apart, Alexia's stomach fluttered with nervous excitement. "Ready to face the music?" she asked, nodding towards the dining room where their parents waited.

Philip took her hand, his touch reassuring. "Together," he said with a smile.

They walked into the warmth of the dining room, the aroma of roasted turkey and cinnamon filling the air. Their parents looked up expectantly, conversation pausing.

Alexia took a deep breath. "Mom, Dad, Mr. and Mrs. Bishop...Philip and I have some news."

Philip squeezed her hand. "Alexia and I are together now. As a couple."

For a moment, silence hung in the air. Then, to Alexia's relief, both sets of parents broke into wide smiles.

"Well, it's about time!" Alexia's mother exclaimed, rushing to hug them both.

As congratulations and laughter filled the room, Alexia caught Philip's eye across the table. His gaze, full of love and promise, made her heart soar. Whatever challenges lay ahead, she knew they would face them side by side, their love as enduring as the evergreen trees that had brought them together.

Alexia sighed, her breath fogging the window of her high-rise apartment as she gazed out at the city skyline. The twinkling lights reminded her of the Christmas trees back home, and a pang of longing squeezed her heart. She turned away from the view, reaching for her phone as it lit up with an incoming FaceTime call.

Philip's smiling face filled the screen, his green eyes crinkling at the corners. "Hey, beautiful," he said warmly. "How was your day?"

"Better now," Alexia replied, sinking into her plush armchair. "The office was chaos, but I managed to nail that presentation I was worried about."

"That's my girl," Philip beamed. "I knew you'd knock it out of the park."

As they chatted, Alexia found herself studying the background behind Philip—the cozy living room of his farmhouse, with its crackling fireplace and rustic wooden beams. She could almost smell the scent of pine needles and cinnamon that always seemed to linger in the air there.

"I miss you," she blurted out suddenly, surprising herself with the intensity of her emotion.

Philip's expression softened. "I miss you too, Lex. More than you know. But hey, only three more weeks until your next visit, right?"

Alexia nodded, trying to shake off the melancholy. "Right. I can't wait to see you in person again."

As they continued talking, Alexia couldn't help but wonder how long they could sustain this long-distance arrangement. The thought of being apart from Philip made her heart ache, but the idea of leaving her career behind was equally daunting. She pushed the worry aside, focusing instead on Philip's animated description of the new saplings he'd planted that day.

Little did she know that at that very moment, Philip was making plans that would change everything.

Three weeks later, Alexia hurried down the busy city sidewalk, her heels clicking against the pavement. She was running late for a lunch meeting and mentally rehearsing her pitch when a familiar voice called out her name.

"Alexia!"

She froze, certain she must be imagining things. Slowly, she turned around, her eyes widening in disbelief. There, in the middle of the bustling city street, stood Philip, looking slightly out of place in his flannel shirt and work boots.

"Philip?" she gasped. "What are you doing here?"

He grinned, closing the distance between them in a few long strides. "Surprising you," he said, pulling her into a tight embrace.

As they parted, Alexia noticed Philip's hands

were trembling slightly. Before she could ask what was wrong, he took a deep breath and dropped down to one knee right there on the sidewalk.

"Alexia Beasley," he began, his voice thick with emotion, "I love you more than I ever thought possible. Will you marry me?"

Alexia's heart soared, but a flicker of doubt crossed her face. "Philip, I...yes! Of course, yes!" she exclaimed, tears of joy welling in her eyes. As he slipped the ring onto her finger, she couldn't help but ask, "But what about the tree farm? Your family's legacy?"

Philip stood, taking her hands in his. "That's something I wanted to talk to you about. I actually probably should have led with that," he said sheepishly as he guided her to a nearby bench. They sat down, the city bustling around them.

"I spoke with my dad," Philip began, his green eyes shining with a mix of excitement and nervousness. "He agreed to let Uncle Jim take over the day-to-day operations of the farm."

Alexia's brow furrowed in confusion. "But I thought...I mean, it's been in your family for generations."

Philip nodded, a gentle smile playing on his lips. "It has, and it will stay in the family. I'll still inherit it someday, but..." He paused, taking a deep breath. "The truth is, Alexia, my heart's not in it the way it should be. I'll still always be a part of the tree farm, but I want to branch out, try something new. I might try to find more partners for the farm here. See if we can pick up more clients. I don't know yet, but I figured God would guide me."

Alexia felt a mix of emotions wash over her. "You mean...?"

"I want to move to the city," Philip said, his voice filled with determination. "To be with you, to start our life together. I've been thinking about it for a while now, and this feels right."

Alexia's mind raced. "But the farm has always been such a big part of your life."

Philip chuckled softly, reaching out to tuck a strand of her chestnut hair behind her ear. "My dreams have changed, Alexia. You've shown me there's a whole world out there beyond the farm. I want to explore it with you."

Alexia felt tears of happiness threatening to spill over. "Are you sure this is what you want?"

"More sure than I've ever been about anything," Philip replied, his voice steady and warm.

Overwhelmed with emotion, Alexia leaned in, closing the distance between them. Their lips met in a tender, passionate kiss, the world around them fading away. In that moment, surrounded by the hustle and bustle of the city, Alexia and Philip found their own little piece of Christmas magic, a promise of a future filled with love, adventure, and new beginnings.

Excerpt from the next book in the A Very Merry State of Love series

CHRISTMAS IN CONNECTICUT

The crisp December air nipped at Ashley's cheeks as she stepped out of her rental car, her designer boots crunching on the snow-dusted sidewalk. Ridgefield's Main Street stretched before her, a picturesque scene straight out of a Christmas card with twinkling lights and festive wreaths adorning every storefront.

"Well, here goes nothing," Ashley muttered, adjusting her cashmere scarf. She took a deep breath, inhaling the familiar scent of pine and wood smoke that always meant home.

As she strolled down the sidewalk, memories flooded back. There was the ice cream parlor where she'd had her first job, and the old movie theater where she'd shared her first kiss. Each sight tugged at her heart, a bittersweet reminder of simpler times.

"Ashley? Ashley Sampson, is that you?" a cheery voice called out.

Ashley turned to see Mrs. Henderson, her old neighbor, bustling towards her with arms outstretched.

"Mrs. Henderson! It's so good to see you," Ashley replied, embracing the older woman. The warm hug felt like a balm to her frayed nerves.

"My goodness, look at you! All grown up and so sophisticated," Mrs. Henderson beamed. "Are you home for the holidays?"

Ashley nodded, forcing a smile. "Yes, just got in. Thought I'd take a walk down memory lane before heading to my parents'."

"Well, it's wonderful to have you back, dear. We've missed you around here."

As Mrs. Henderson continued chatting, Ashley's gaze drifted to the town square. The massive Christmas tree stood proudly in the center, just as it had every year of her childhood. For a moment, she was transported back to happier times, before the pressures of her career and her recent heartbreak had left her feeling so...lost.

"...and of course, your parents are just tickled to

have you home," Mrs. Henderson was saying. "Your mother's been telling everyone at church about your big promotion."

Ashley's smile faltered slightly. "Oh, yes. It's been...quite a year."

As they said their goodbyes and Ashley continued her walk, she couldn't shake the feeling of being caught between two worlds. The familiar sights and sounds of Ridgefield wrapped around her like a cozy blanket, but the weight of her recent struggles still pressed heavily on her shoulders.

Passing by the old high school, Ashley paused, her hand resting on the cool brick of the building. She closed her eyes, memories washing over her. The laughter of friends, the excitement of first loves, the dreams of the future that had seemed so certain then.

"I used to have it all figured out," she whispered to herself, a rueful smile playing on her lips. "When did everything get so complicated?"

With a deep sigh, Ashley straightened her shoulders and continued down the street. The anxiety of facing her past mingled with a growing sense of hope.

She walked back to the car and got back in.

Time to head to her parents' house.

Ashley's heart skipped a beat as she turned

onto the familiar oak-lined driveway of her childhood home. The porch light was already on, casting a warm glow across the snow-dusted lawn. Before she could even reach for the doorbell, the front door swung open, revealing her mother's beaming face.

"Ashley, sweetheart!" her mom exclaimed, wrapping her in a tight embrace. "Oh, we've missed you so much!"

The comforting scents of home enveloped Ashley as she stepped inside, the tension in her shoulders easing slightly. "I've missed you too, Mom," she said, her voice thick with emotion.

Her father appeared from the living room, his kind eyes crinkling at the corners as he smiled. "There's our girl," he said, pulling her into a bear hug.

As they settled in the cozy kitchen, steaming mugs of hot cocoa in hand, Ashley could feel her parents' concerned gazes. She traced the rim of her mug, avoiding eye contact.

"Honey," her mom began gently, "we know this year hasn't been easy for you. With the breakup and all..."

Ashley's chest tightened. "I'm fine, really," she insisted, forcing a smile. "Work's been great, and-"

"Ash," her father interrupted softly, "it's okay not to be okay. We just want you to be happy again."

Tears pricked at Ashley's eyes. "I know, Dad. I'm trying. I just...I thought I had it all figured out, you know?"

Her mother reached across the table, squeezing her hand. "Sometimes God has other plans, sweetie. But that doesn't mean you won't find happiness again."

As Ashley nodded, wiping away a stray tear, the doorbell chimed. Her father's eyes lit up. "Ah, that must be Myles! I invited him over for dinner."

Ashley's heart stuttered. "Myles? As in Myles Hickman?"

Her mother's smile was knowing. "You two have a lot of catching up to do."

Moments later, Ashley found herself face-to-face with her childhood best friend. Myles stood in the doorway, snowflakes clinging to his broad shoulders, his warm smile sending a flutter through her chest.

"Hey, Ash," he said, his voice as soothing as she remembered. "Long time no see."

As they sat down to dinner, the conversation flowed easily, filled with laughter and shared memories. Ashley found herself relaxing, drawn in by Myles's gentle humor and attentive gaze.

"So, you're a big-shot ad exec now," Myles teased, his eyes twinkling. "Always knew you'd make it big."

Ashley chuckled, feeling a blush creep up her cheeks. "And you're Ridgefield's master carpenter. I've heard about your work around town."

Myles shrugged modestly. "Just doing what I love. Speaking of which, how are you really doing, Ash? Your mom mentioned things have been tough..."

For a moment, Ashley hesitated, caught off guard by the genuine concern in his voice. She met his gaze, finding nothing but warmth and understanding there.

"I'm...getting there," she admitted softly. "It's been a journey."

Myles nodded, his hand briefly touching hers. "Well, you've got a whole town rooting for you. And I'm always here if you need a friend."

As their eyes met, Ashley felt a familiar spark, one she thought she'd left behind years ago. She smiled, realizing that coming home might just be the fresh start she needed.

Ashley ran her fingers along the dusty cardboard box, her heart quickening as she recognized her own teenage handwriting scrawled across the side: "Memories—Do Not Open!"

She laughed softly, shaking her head at her dramatic younger self. "Well, past Ashley, I think it's time we break that rule."

Settling cross-legged on her childhood bedroom floor, she carefully lifted the lid. A wave of nostalgia hit her as she pulled out a faded Ridgefield High yearbook.

"Oh my goodness," she whispered, flipping through the pages. Her eyes landed on a photo of herself and Myles at the senior prom. They were both grinning, his arm draped casually over her shoulders.

Ashley's throat tightened. "We were so young," she murmured, tracing Myles's face with her fingertip.

She set the yearbook aside, reaching deeper into the box. Her hand closed around a small, wooden ornament—a delicately carved Christmas tree.

"I can't believe I still have this," Ashley breathed, turning it over in her palm. Memories flooded back—Myles presenting it to her on their last Christmas before college, his eyes shining with pride at his handiwork.

She closed her eyes, remembering his words: "So you'll always have a piece of Ridgefield with you, no matter where life takes you."

Opening her eyes, Ashley felt a tear slip down her cheek. She wiped it away, surprised by the intensity of emotion washing over her.

"What am I doing?" she asked herself softly, staring at the ornament.

She stood, walking to the window. The twinkling lights of Ridgefield stretched out before her, warm and inviting. In the distance, she could just make out the steeple of the old church where she and Myles had shared their first kiss.

He'd been her first boyfriend, but life had pulled them in different directions.

She was glad they could at least still be friends. Theirs hadn't been a bitter break-up. They'd simply gone in different directions.

Now Ashley wondered why.

About the Author

Award-winning author Kayla Lowe writes women's fiction that explores complex themes with sensitivity and depth. Kayla's books delve into the intricacies of relationships, self-discovery, and resilience. From cozy love stories interspersed with a bit of faith to heartwarming tales of friendship and suspenseful novels of empowerment and heartbreak, her books illustrate the struggles specific to women.

When she's not churning out her next novel, you can find her with her feet in the sand and a book in her hand or curled up on the couch with her dogs.

Visit her website at www.authorkaylalowe.com.

Also by Kayla Lowe

Series

Christmas Blessings

Christmas Miracle for Two

A Christmas Promise of Love

A Christmas of Renewed Faith

Women of the Bible Fiction

Ruth

Esther

Rachel

Hannah

Deborah

Charms of the Chaste Court

A Courtship in Covent Garden

Whispers in Westminster

Romance in Regent's Park

Serenade on Strand Street

Treasure in Tower Bridge

Sweet Honey by the Sea

The Beekeeper's Secret (Book 1)

A Royal Honeycomb (Book 2)

Bees in Blossom (Book 3)

Honeyed Kisses (Book 4)

Blooming Forever (Book 5)

Strawberry Beach Series

Beachside Lessons (Book 1)

Beachside Lessons (Book 2)

Beachside Lessons (Book 3)

Panama City Beach Series

Sun-Kissed Secrets (Book 1)

Sun-Kissed Secrets (Book 2)

Sun-Kissed Secrets (Book 3)

The Tainted Love Saga

Of Love and Deception (Book 1)

Of Love and Family (Book 2)

Of Love and Violence (Book 3)

Of Love and Abuse(Book 4)

Of Love and Crime (Book 5)

Of Love and Addiction (Book 6)

Of Love and Redemption (Book 7)

<u>Standalones</u>

Maiden's Blush

<u>Poetry</u>

Phantom Poetry

Lost and Found

www.ingramcontent.com/pod-product-compliance
Lightning Source LLC
LaVergne TN
LVHW040906150826
845672LV00007B/1920

* 9 7 9 8 2 3 0 0 2 1 4 9 0 *